WALT DISNEY
Dumbo

TWIN
BOOKS

GALLERY BOOKS
An imprint of W.H. Smith Publishers Inc.
112 Madison Avenue
New York, New York 10016

2

Early one morning while most people were still fast asleep, a group of storks appeared in the sky. They had been flying all night and were very happy to catch a glimpse of a large tent surrounded by a group of smaller tents and trailers.

"There, below, there's the circus!" shouted one of the storks as he released his bundle. Soon all the other storks let go of their parcels and the sky was filled with parachutes carrying blue and pink bundles. A gentle breeze delivered the drifting arrivals right to the tents.

Being the tallest, Mrs Giraffe was the first to spot the bundles. "Wake up everyone! The storks have come," she called. "Our little ones are here!"

Baby giraffes, tigers, hippopotami, bears and kangaroos floated down to their waiting mothers. The animals ran this way and that to catch their young. A little lion cub was tangled up in a tree, but Mrs Giraffe soon had him out and into his mother's arms.

4

Mrs Jumbo, the elephant, watched as one after another of the little animals arrived. Even after the sky was empty, she continued to search, straining her neck in all directions.

"Oh dear," she sighed. "I was certain that there would be a bundle for me. Now I'll have to wait until next year." She began to cry.

5

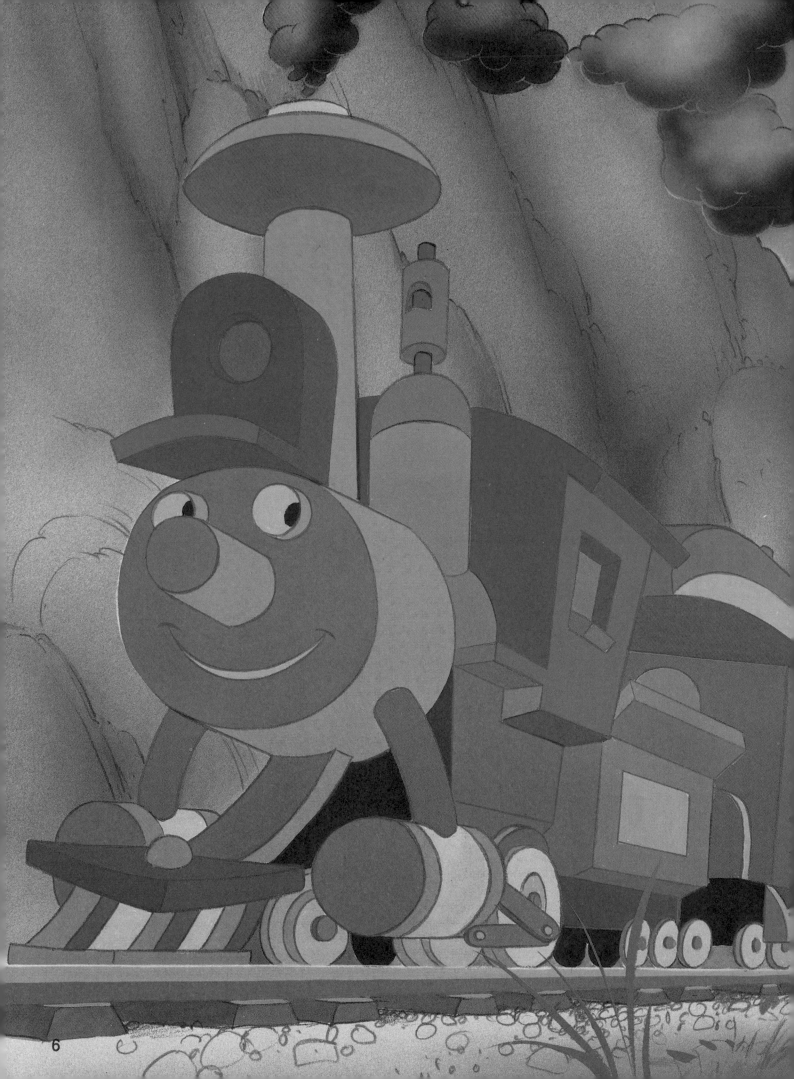

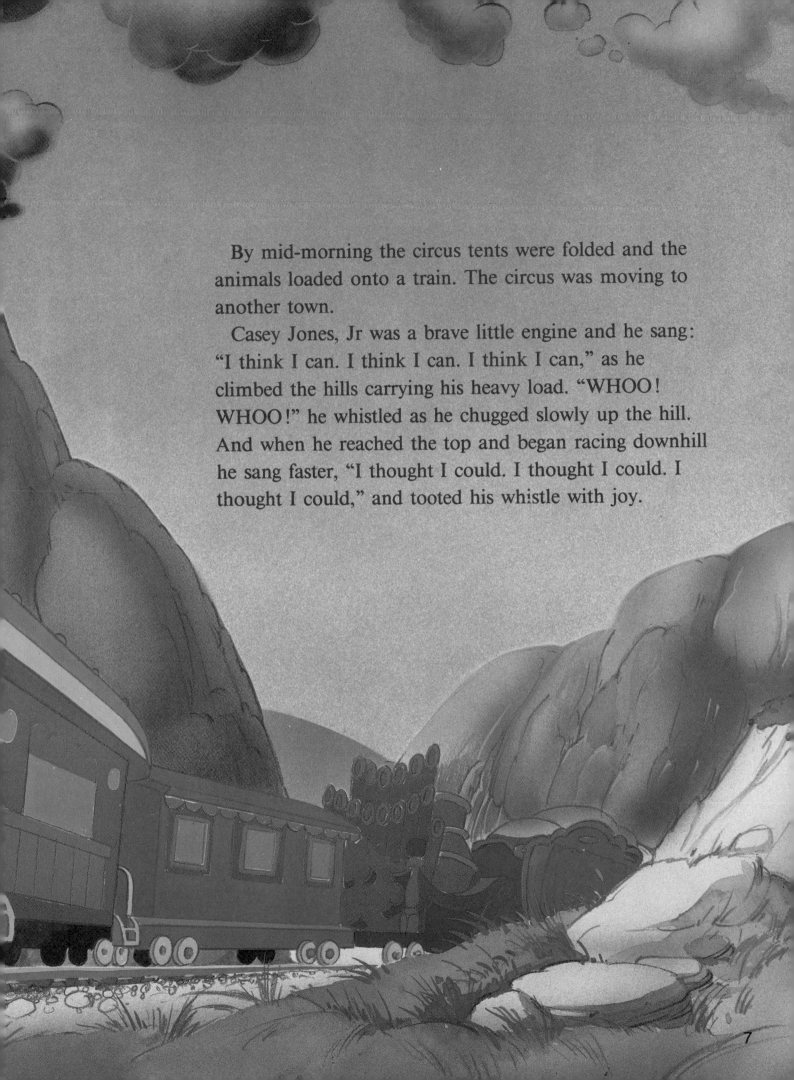

By mid-morning the circus tents were folded and the animals loaded onto a train. The circus was moving to another town.

Casey Jones, Jr was a brave little engine and he sang: "I think I can. I think I can. I think I can," as he climbed the hills carrying his heavy load. "WHOO! WHOO!" he whistled as he chugged slowly up the hill. And when he reached the top and began racing downhill he sang faster, "I thought I could. I thought I could. I thought I could," and tooted his whistle with joy.

As the train sped along the tracks, a small shape moved along on top of the cars. It was a stork, carrying a large bundle and shouting, "Mrs Jumbo! Special delivery for Mrs Jumbo!"

Hearing the stork's shouts, two of the elephants stuck their trunks through an opening and waved. "Over here," signalled another with her trunk.

9

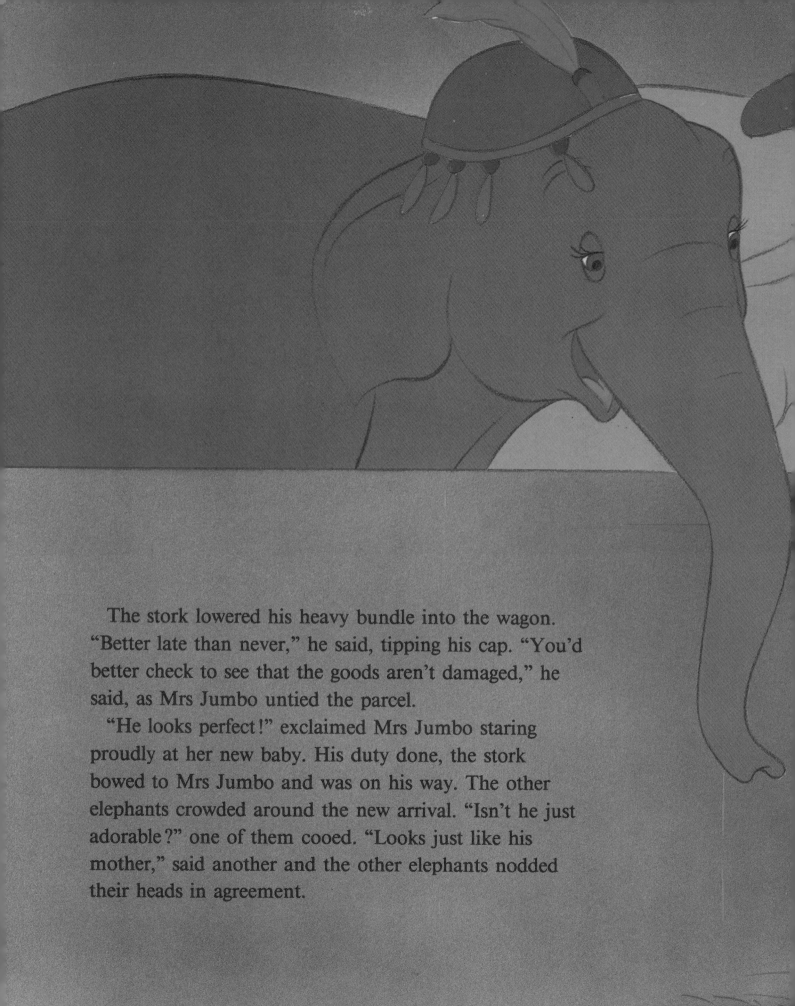

The stork lowered his heavy bundle into the wagon. "Better late than never," he said, tipping his cap. "You'd better check to see that the goods aren't damaged," he said, as Mrs Jumbo untied the parcel.

"He looks perfect!" exclaimed Mrs Jumbo staring proudly at her new baby. His duty done, the stork bowed to Mrs Jumbo and was on his way. The other elephants crowded around the new arrival. "Isn't he just adorable?" one of them cooed. "Looks just like his mother," said another and the other elephants nodded their heads in agreement.

All this attention was too much for the little one. And letting out a big sneeze, he shook his head, exposing two enormous floppy ears.

"Take a look at those ears," said one of the elephants, stretching the ear with her trunk.

"It's too bad that the stork has already left," sniggered another. "You should file a complaint for damaged goods." The elephants all began to laugh.

"I never saw anything so dumb-looking in all my life. We'll have to call him Dumbo," said the biggest elephant, causing more laughter.

Mrs Jumbo picked up her
baby and stalked off to a
corner.

"Don't pay any attention
to them," she said softly.
"I think you are the
handsomest elephant in the
world. They're just jealous.
And to show them I don't
care what they say, I will call
you Dumbo after all!"

Late that night the train
finally reached the town
where the circus was to
perform. The animals were
unloaded and the tents were
pitched.

16

The next morning a parade was held to announce the circus's arrival. Proud camels led the way, followed by the ringmaster who shouted to the crowd, "Ladies and gentlemen! Boys and girls! Come to the big top tonight! We'll make you laugh! We'll make you cry! You'll see feats of danger that will make you tremble with fear! All this and more at the circus!"

Behind the ringmaster was Happy the Hippo, yawning as he hauled the 33-ton pipe organ along.

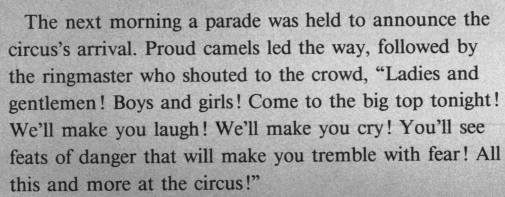

An endless stream of animals passed through the town. Kangaroos carried their babies in their pouches and hopped along beside bears, while lions roared from their cages, frightening the crowd.

Bringing up the rear were the elephants, and last of all was little Dumbo. Clutching his mother's tail, Dumbo looked around in wonder. This was his first parade and his eyes were round with excitement. He dreamed of the day when he would be at the head of the parade.

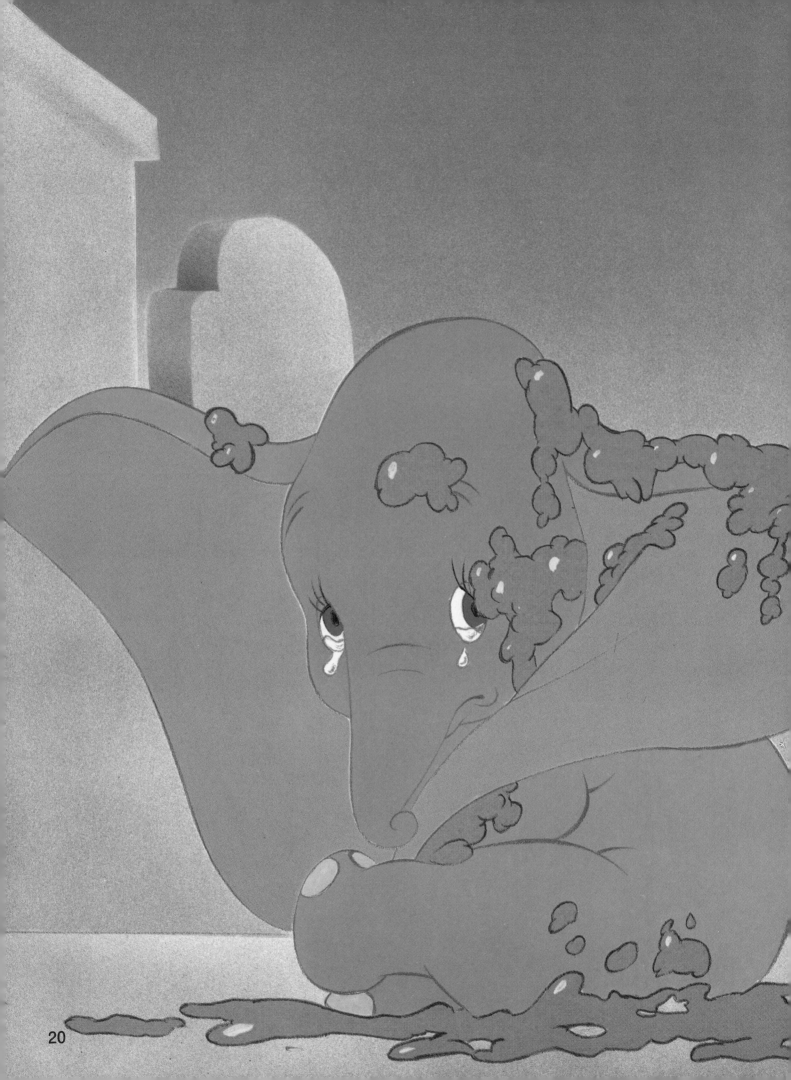

Lost in his daydreams, Dumbo did not look where he was going. He stepped on one of his ears and tumbled headfirst into a mud puddle. Seeing the little elephant trip over his ears, the crowd began to laugh.

"Look at him!" a boy shouted. "With ears like those, he must be Batman!"

"He may be blind, but with those big ears he can't possibly be deaf," cried another boy, causing the crowd to laugh and jeer even more.

Dumbo was filled with shame and desperately tried to hide his ears. Tears fell as he unsuccessfully folded his ears about him.

A bold little boy walked up to Dumbo and pulled one
of his ears. Dumbo cried out in pain. Hearing her little
one cry out, Mrs Jumbo rushed to his aid, trumpeting
in anger. She grabbed the naughty boy with her trunk
and lifted him into the air. "This will teach you to pick
on a defenseless little elephant," she snorted.

"Help! Help!" shouted the little boy, who was not so
brave when he was dangling in the air.

But, since Mrs Jumbo had only wanted to teach him a
lesson, she placed him gently back on the ground.

But the crowd had become hysterical. Thinking that Mrs Jumbo was wild, they called for help. "That elephant is crazy! Do something; she's dangerous!" shouted the bystanders.

The trainers came running with ropes which they lassooed around Mrs Jumbo's neck.

Mrs Jumbo reared up on her hind legs and shrieked in protest, but it was too late. The ropes tightened around her and she was led away. "Lock her up!" shouted the ringmaster.

Poor little Dumbo looked on in shock. There was nothing that he could do to rescue his mother.

Dumbo looked for the other elephants, hoping to find out where his mother was being held. But when the elephants saw Dumbo coming they turned their backs on him.

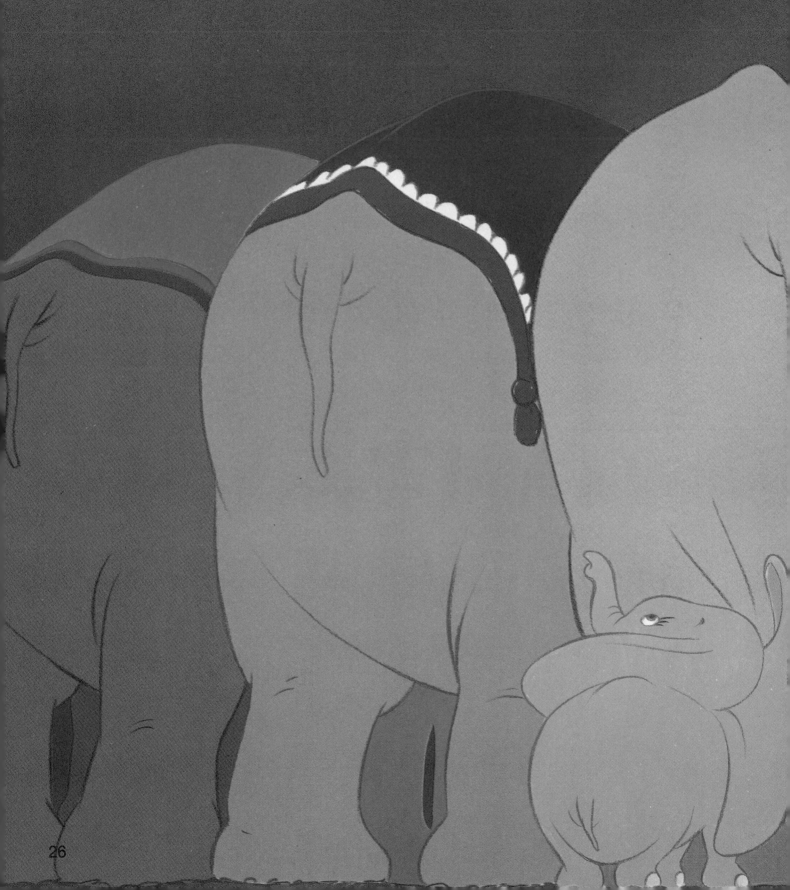

"What a disgrace. All that fuss for a floppy-eared imbecile," said one of elephants.

"Nothing would have happened if it weren't for that Dumbo! It's all his fault," replied another.

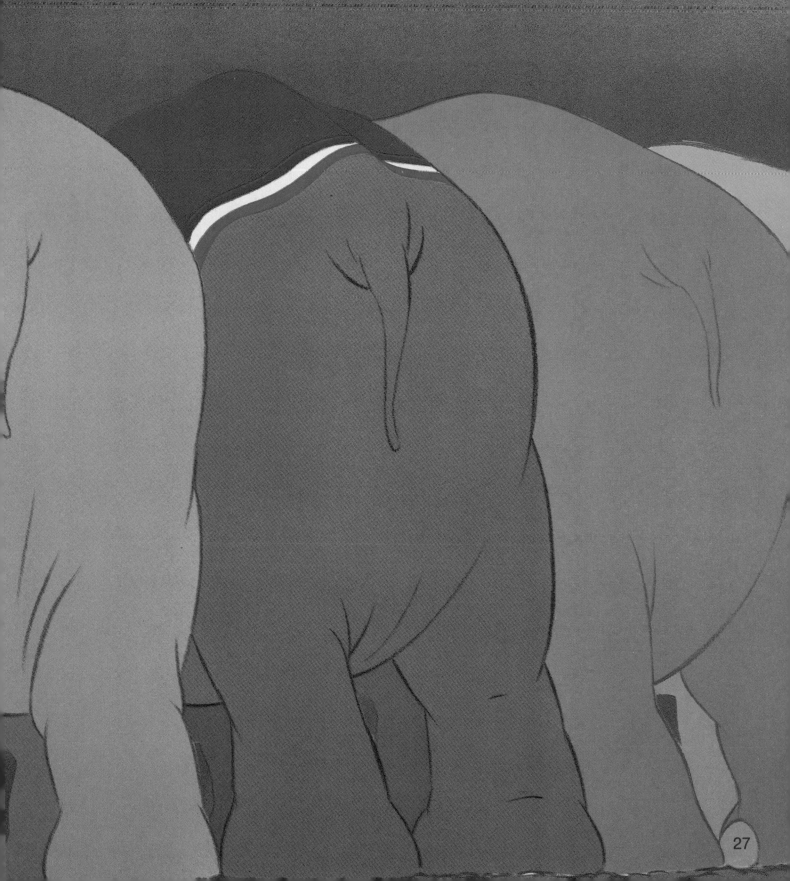

Poor Dumbo sat down and began to cry. As he sobbed quietly in his corner, he felt something tickling his trunk. It was a little mouse.

"Don't be afraid, Dumbo. I'm your friend," whispered the little mouse. "I heard what they said about you and I'm going to teach those gossiping pachyderms a lesson."

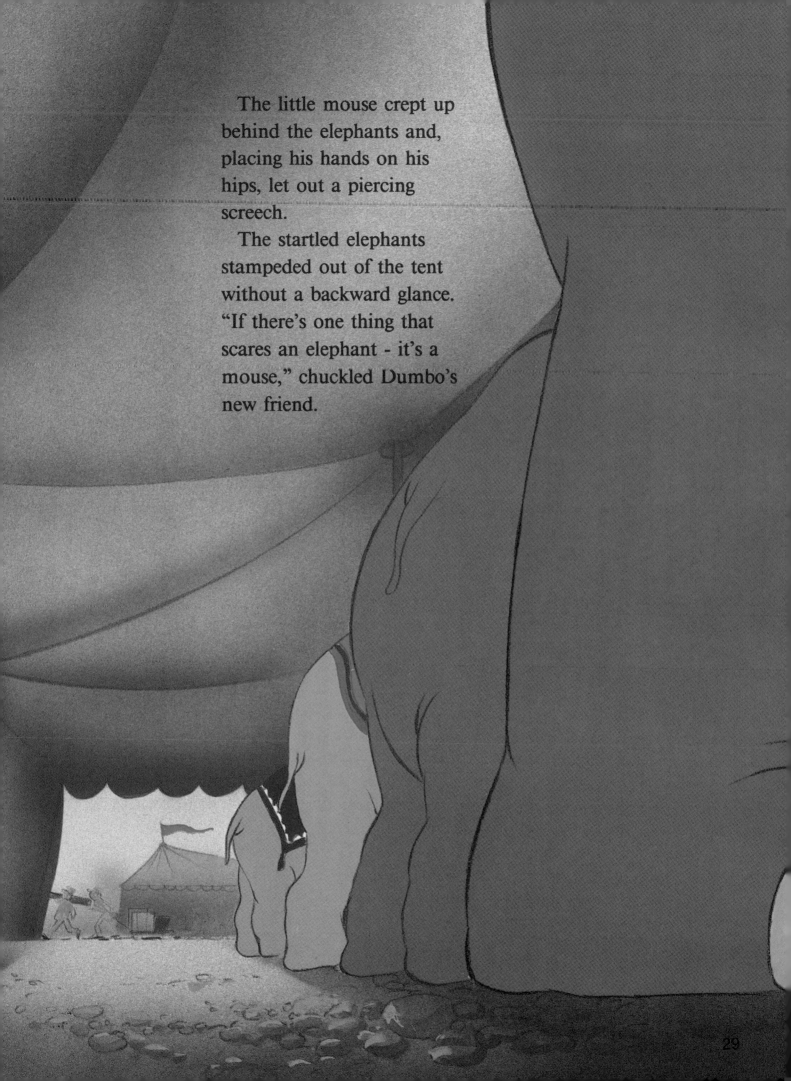

The little mouse crept up behind the elephants and, placing his hands on his hips, let out a piercing screech.

The startled elephants stampeded out of the tent without a backward glance. "If there's one thing that scares an elephant - it's a mouse," chuckled Dumbo's new friend.

Dumbo looked at the little mouse with admiration. The mouse bowed. "Timothy's the name," he said. "I may be small, but don't let my size fool you. I get around and no one notices me. I know everything that goes on in this circus. I know that your mother's been locked away, and I also know that you're ashamed of your ears. Well, I think they're great. Those ears are going to make you famous one of these days. Stick with me kid, I've got big plans for you."

And so Dumbo found a friend in the shape of a sassy little mouse.

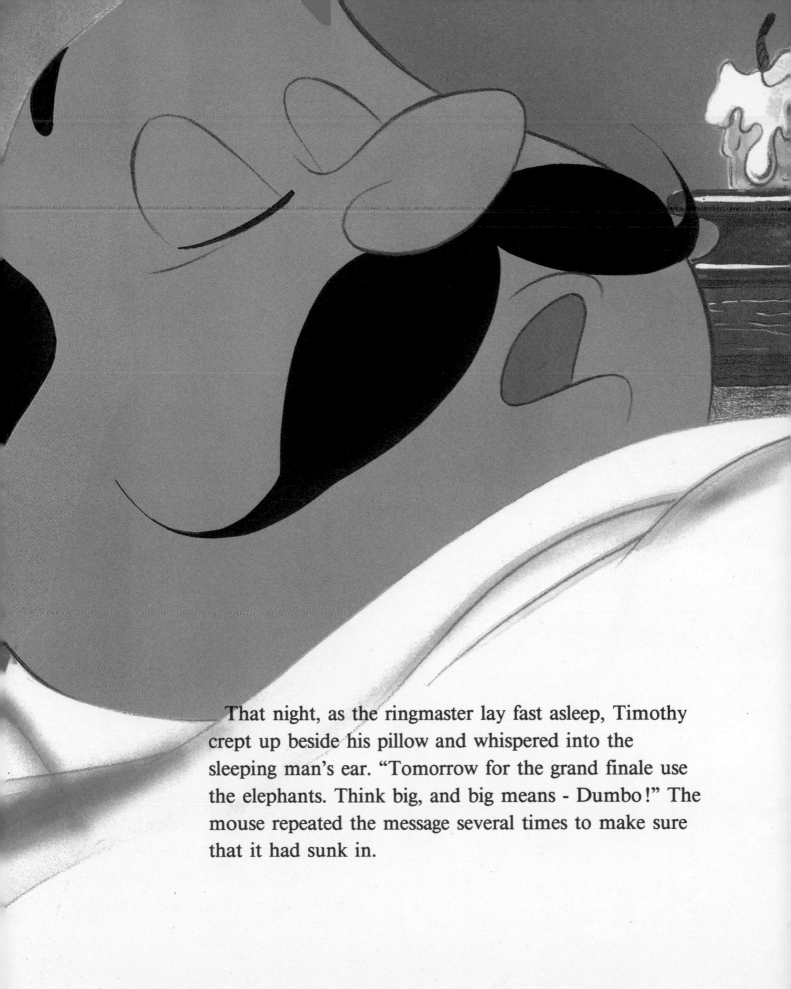

That night, as the ringmaster lay fast asleep, Timothy crept up beside his pillow and whispered into the sleeping man's ear. "Tomorrow for the grand finale use the elephants. Think big, and big means - Dumbo!" The mouse repeated the message several times to make sure that it had sunk in.

The next morning the ring-master awoke with a smile on his face. "I've had a wonderful idea for the new grand finale," he said. "I'll use the elephants and that little Dumbo, too. And to think that I thought of it all by myself." With that, he rushed off to prepare the new act.

That night standing under the spotlight, surrounded by elephants balancing on their hind legs, the ringmaster announced the grand finale.

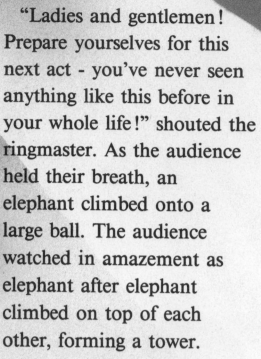

"Ladies and gentlemen! Prepare yourselves for this next act - you've never seen anything like this before in your whole life!" shouted the ringmaster. As the audience held their breath, an elephant climbed onto a large ball. The audience watched in amazement as elephant after elephant climbed on top of each other, forming a tower.

"Ouch! Take your foot out of my eye," grumbled the elephant on the bottom.

"I thought you said you were going on a diet," mumbled another elephant, drooping under the weight of her friend.

"And now for the finishing touch!" cried the ringmaster. "Dumbo is going to leap from the trampoline onto the top of this mountain of elephants." The ringmaster signalled for a drumroll.

The spotlight shone on the wings where Dumbo was frozen with stage fright. Timothy, the mouse, had tied Dumbo's ears back out of the way. He gave Dumbo a nudge and whispered, "Go ahead kid. Show them what you're made of."

Dumbo gathered up his courage and began to run into the big ring. As he ran, his ears came untied and flopped down. The audience gasped as Dumbo tripped and went flying head-over-heels, bumping right into the ball on which the elephants were precariously balanced.

For a split second all was silent, and then a faint creaking could be heard as the elephants began to sway back and forth. The audience fled for their lives, while the huge tower of elephants began to fall. Within seconds panic had broken loose.

One of the falling elephants landed on the trapeze and another clung to her tail. Back and forth they swung. "I can't hold on much longer," shouted the elephant who was holding on by her trunk.

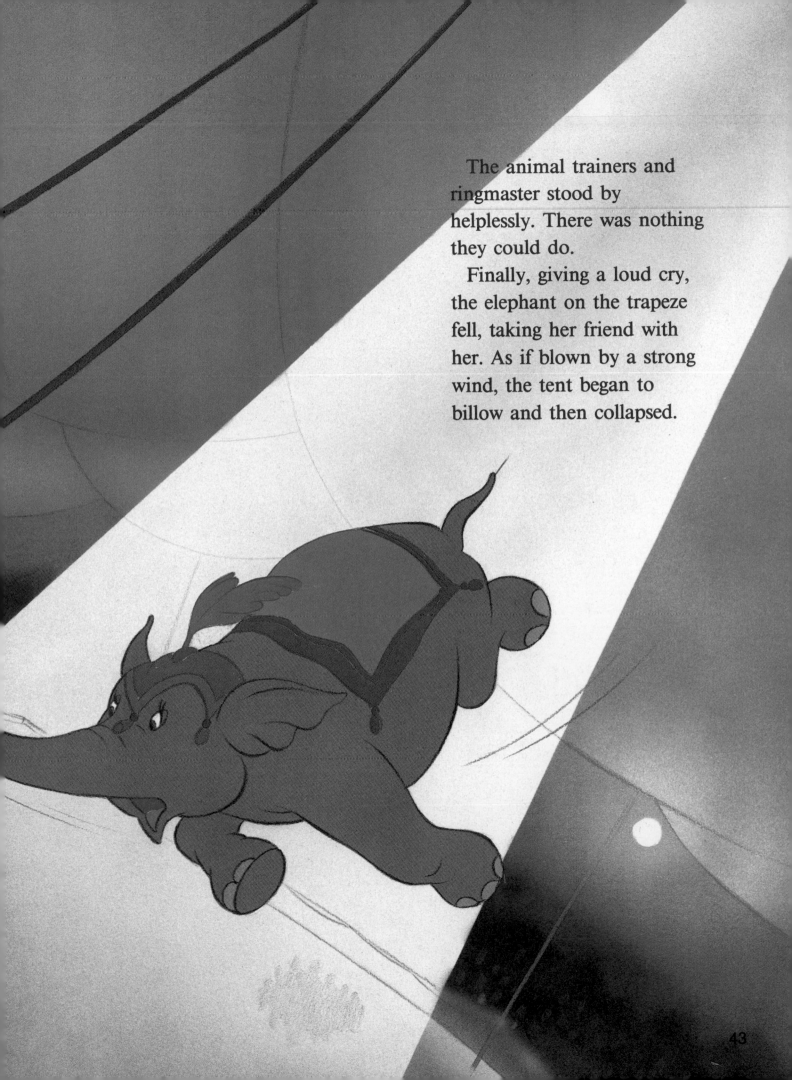

The animal trainers and ringmaster stood by helplessly. There was nothing they could do.

Finally, giving a loud cry, the elephant on the trapeze fell, taking her friend with her. As if blown by a strong wind, the tent began to billow and then collapsed.

Fortunately, except for a few bumps and bruises, no one had been badly hurt. Dumbo, however, was in serious trouble.

"A star! Huh!" screamed the ringmaster. "You're nothing but a bumbling, bungling clown! And, since that's all you're good for, that's exactly what you'll be!"

Dumbo's face was painted and he was forced to stand
in the ring waving a little flag. Night after night Dumbo
was forced to play the fool as clowns threw cream pies
in his face, while the audience laughed and jeered.

46

One day the clowns came up with a new act for Dumbo. A large house was erected with a make-believe fire. At the very top was Dumbo dressed up as a big baby in a bonnet.

Dressed as firemen the clowns ran around frantically waving fire hoses and squirting everything. One clown held up a tiny ladder. "Do you think this is long enough?" he asked, as the audience roared with laughter.

"That ladder is much too short," shouted one of the clowns. "The baby will have to jump!"

"Jump, baby! We'll catch you," screamed the firemen, who were holding a safety-net.

Dumbo looked down, shaking with fright. It was a long way down and the net didn't look very strong. The fumes from the make-believe fire hurt his eyes. The audience began to chant, "Jump! Jump!"

Dumbo closed his eyes and leaped into the air. His ears flapped out behind him.

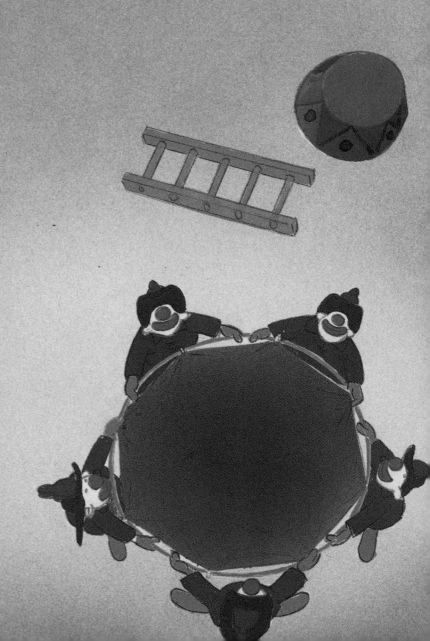

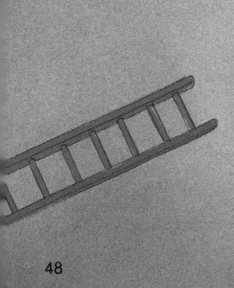

Dumbo opened his eyes and saw the net below him. But his ordeal wasn't over. The net tore under his weight and Dumbo fell into a tub of water, making a big SPLASH!

The audience roared with laughter at the sight of the big, wet baby. Soon the laughter turned into applause, but the clowns alone took their bows. Ashamed and still shaking, Dumbo slunk off to a corner. He had never felt so miserable in his life.

Timothy Mouse found Dumbo shivering in the corner. "What you need is a good rubdown and you'll be in shape in no time," said Timothy, taking up a sponge and scrubbing off the make-up. "Cheer up Dumbo! I've got some good news for you. I've found out where they're keeping your mother. Tonight at midnight I'll take you to her." And before Dumbo knew it, Timothy was gone.

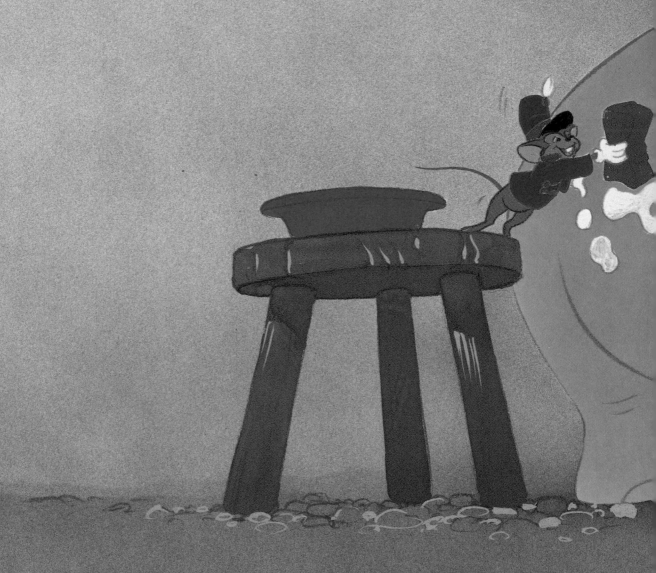

That night as the town clocks struck midnight, Mrs Jumbo heard a noise outside her cell. She turned her head and saw a little trunk sticking through the bars. "Dumbo, is that you?" she whispered, moving slowly towards the door. Enormous balls and chains were attached to her legs, making it difficult to move. "Wait there, I'm coming," she said, as she dragged the heavy balls, trying to make as little noise as possible.

Mrs Jumbo slid her trunk between the bars and touched Dumbo. Her eyes filled with tears. "You've grown since I saw you last," she said, cradling Dumbo in her trunk. "And you smell nice and sweet. Thank goodness someone is looking after you." Rocking Dumbo gently, she began to sing a lullaby.

After some time, Timothy appeared and whispered to Dumbo that it was time to go. Dumbo reluctantly said good night to his mother and left with Timothy.

As they neared the circus tents, Dumbo and Timothy heard shrieks of laughter and the popping of champagne corks. The noise was coming from the clowns' tent. They were celebrating the success of their act.

"Did you catch the look on that little idiot's face when he fell into the water?" asked one of the clowns, collapsing in a fit of giggles.

"Tomorrow we'll make the house taller. That will make an even bigger splash," said another clown.

Just then, one of the champagne bottles fell through the flap and into a pail outside the tent. The clowns were too drunk to notice.

"Come on Dumbo," said Timothy. "You deserve the champagne as much as they do. Let's drink a toast to your great future."

Dumbo plunged his trunk into the pail and took a great gulp. In his excitement, Timothy pitched over and fell into the pail.

The champagne began to take effect. Dumbo slumped on the ground and began blowing bubbles, while Timothy giggled and sang.

Dumbo's eyelids began to feel heavy and soon he was fast asleep, with strange shapes floating in his dreams. Pink and purple elephants danced and performed tricks. Dumbo had the sensation that he was flying. He could even hear birds.

Early next morning a gang of crows gathered around the sleeping Dumbo and Timothy.

"Will ya look at that giant? Never thought I'd see the day when elephants lived in trees!" exclaimed a cigar-smoking crow.

"What I wanna know," said one of the other crows, "is how did he get up here?"

"How do you think he got here? He flew!" replied the chief crow.

"Flew!" shouted the others. "Elephants can't fly!"

Dumbo, who was half asleep, smelled the cigar smoke and thought that he was dreaming. "Oh, not the clowns again," he murmured, rolling over onto his side. But Dumbo was not dreaming and in turning over, he lost his balance and began to fall out of the tree.

It was too late to grab on to the branches. Down he went, landing in a stream with an enormous SPLASH!

Timothy, too, came spilling out of the tree and landed with a tiny PLOP! in the stream.

The sight of Dumbo and Timothy falling into the
stream was too much for the crows, and bursting with
laughter they began to sing.

"Did you ever see an elephant fly?" sang Dandy Crow.

"Well, I've seen a horse fly," said the Preacher Crow.

"I've seen a peanut stand and heard a rubber band.
I've seen a needle that winked its eye.
I've seen a front porch swing and heard a diamond ring.
But I ain't never seen an elephant fly.
But I ain't never seen an elephant fly."

But Timothy was not amused. "What's so funny about a poor little elephant falling out of a tree?" he demanded. Then suddenly he stopped and scratched his head. "How did he get up into the tree?" he wondered aloud.

The crows all spoke at once, "he flew."

"FLEW!" Timothy shouted, turning to look at Dumbo in amazement.

Dumbo blinked his eyes and stared at the crows.

Dumbo remembered his dream and how he had felt as if he was flying, but that was only a dream.

"There's only one way to find out if he can fly, and that's to try," suggested the wise old crow.

"Why not?" said Timothy. "I always said you were special. Come on, Dumbo. Let's give it a try."

Dumbo was not as confident as his friend. He'd had too many falls lately, and wasn't eager to take another.

"Here, take this magic feather," said the wise old crow. "There's a cliff nearby, he can jump from there."

When they reached the cliff, Dumbo took one look down and began to back away. The crows decided that a friendly push was needed. Together they gave a shove, yelling "Heave ho - off you go!"

Dumbo closed his eyes and
began to flap his ears with
all his might. And, instead of
falling through the air, he
began to float.

Timothy gave a shout of
delight. "I knew you could
do it! Look! We're flying."

Dumbo opened one eye
and then the other. Timothy
was right. He wasn't falling,
he was gliding like a bird.

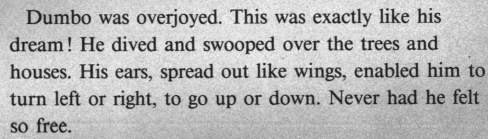

Dumbo was overjoyed. This was exactly like his dream! He dived and swooped over the trees and houses. His ears, spread out like wings, enabled him to turn left or right, to go up or down. Never had he felt so free.

Timothy began chattering away. "Just wait until the others see you! Oh, Dumbo, I just knew you were headed for big things. But we mustn't let the others know just yet. Wait until tonight - we'll give them a big surprise."

During the circus performance later that day, Dumbo went through the jumping baby routine with Timothy perched on his hat. The clowns had made the burning house even taller. They were looking forward to the enormous splash that Dumbo would make when he fell into the tub.

"Go on, jump!" they yelled.

This time, Dumbo was not afraid. He was carrying his magic feather.

Dumbo jumped into the air, but in his excitement he dropped the feather. Frozen with fear, he began to fall, but Timothy shouted, "That feather isn't magic! You don't need it to fly, Dumbo, you can fly all by yourself."

Hearing Timothy's words, Dumbo spread his ears and flapped them with all his might. Just as he was within a few feet of the safety net, he changed direction. Instead of plunging into the water, he soared up toward the ceiling of the tent.

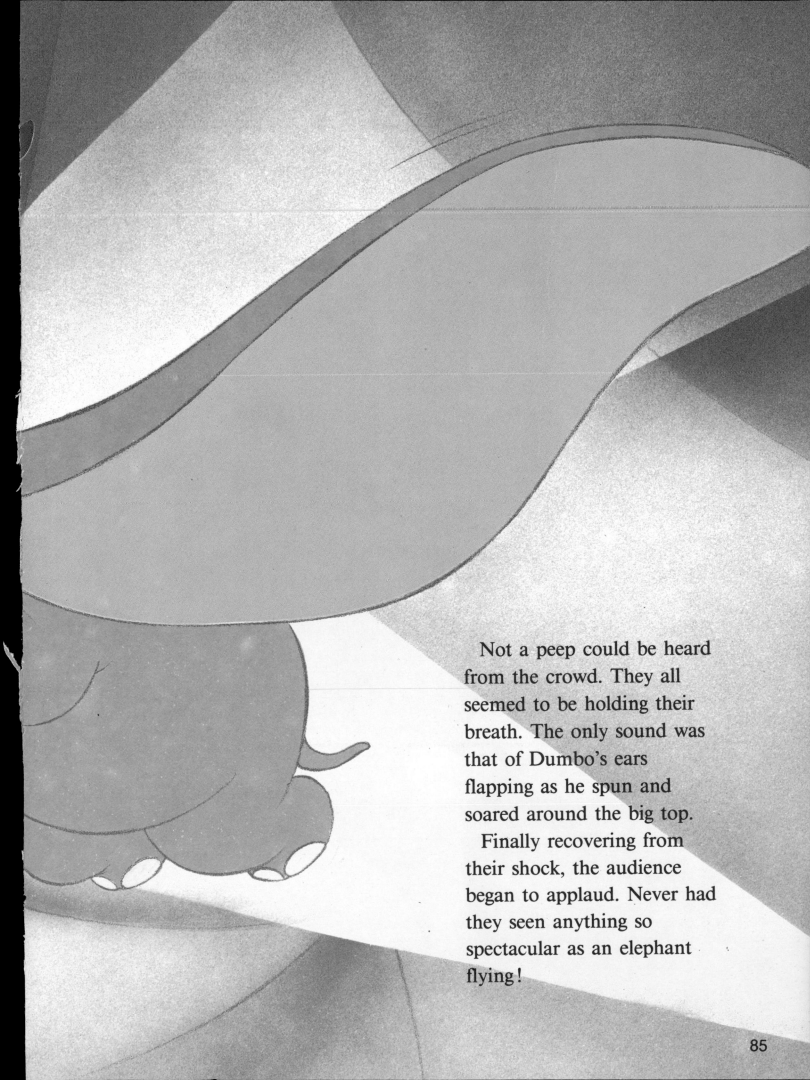

Not a peep could be heard from the crowd. They all seemed to be holding their breath. The only sound was that of Dumbo's ears flapping as he spun and soared around the big top.

Finally recovering from their shock, the audience began to applaud. Never had they seen anything so spectacular as an elephant flying!

Dumbo decided to have some fun and began doing nose dives over the clowns and ringmaster. The audience roared with laughter, but this time at the clowns not at Dumbo. The terrified ringmaster jumped headfirst into the tub of water and Dumbo had his revenge.

Thunderous applause rang in Dumbo's ears as he took his bow in the center ring. Now he was the star of the circus.

Dumbo became an overnight sensation. Every newspaper in the land carried his picture on the front page.

From the Eskimos in Alaska to the Aborigines of Australia, Dumbo's fame was known to all.

In each new <u>town</u> and village
that the circus passed, it was
Dumbo who drew the
crowds. The ringmaster
never stopped boasting about
his new star, shouting "The
greatest, the most earth-
shaking, breathtaking,
fantastical event - Dumbo the
flying elephant!"

Every morning, high above the circus tents, a small figure could be seen soaring about in the sky. It was Dumbo, practicing his act. With Timothy the mouse in his cap, he performed nose dives, spirals, loop-the-loops, spins, rolls and landings, all with his mother proudly watching from a place of honor.

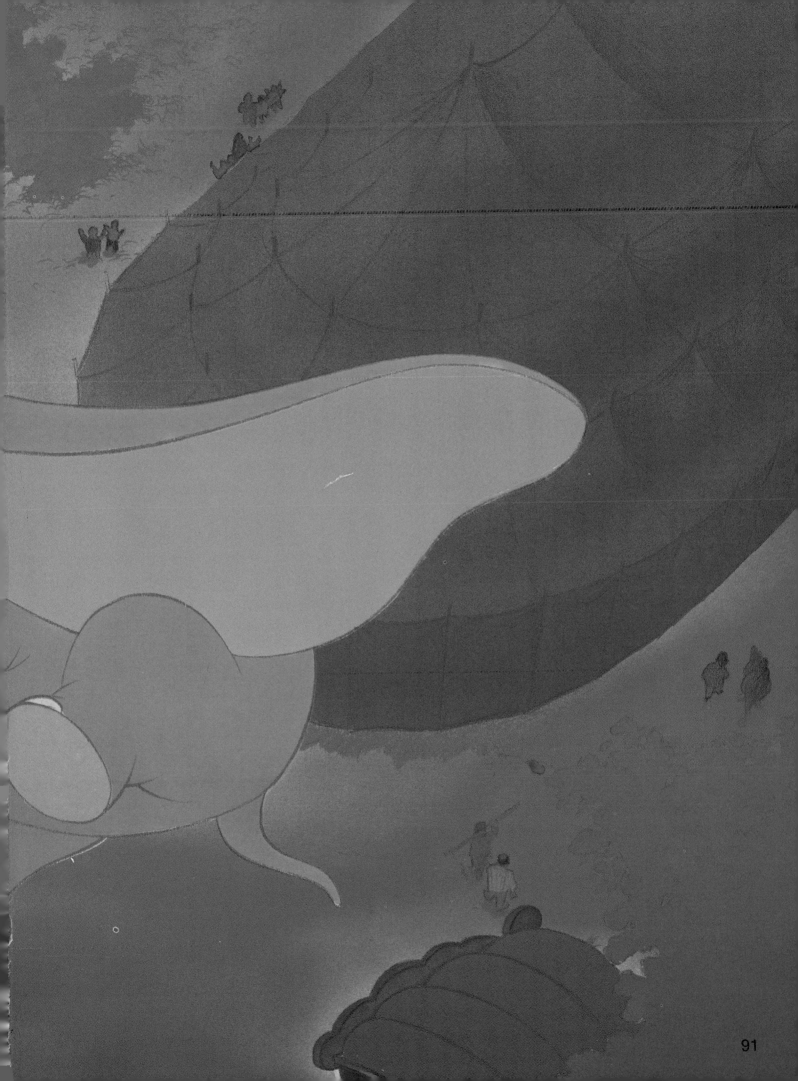

Below, the other elephants looked on with pride. They had quickly changed their attitude towards the "little imbecile."

"He's going to go far, that little one," said one of the elephants.

"I always said that he was special," said another.

"No, I was the first to say that" said yet another, and they would argue on and on.

"WHOO! WHOO! Chuga-Chuga-Chuga-Chuga!" Casey Jones, Jr tooted his whistle with joy between towns. He was very proud of his passenger - Dumbo the flying elephant.

Published by
Gallery Books
A Division of W H Smith Publisher Inc,
112 Madison Avenue
New York, New York 10016
USA

Produced by
Twin Books
15 Sherwood Place
Greenwich, CT. 06830.
USA

ISBN 0-8317-2463-3

Printed in Hong Kong

1 2 3 4 5 6 7 8 9 10